Oscar
needs a
Friend

by Joan Stimson

Illustrated by Meg Rutherford

BARRON'S

First edition for the United States and Canada
published 1998 by Barron's Educational Series, Inc.

Text copyright © 1998 by Joan Stimson
Illustrations © 1998 by Meg Rutherford

First published in the UK by
Scholastic Ltd. 1998

All inquiries should be addressed to:
Barron's Educational Series, Inc.
250 Wireless Boulevard
Hauppauge, New York 11788

http://www.barronseduc.com

Library of Congress Catalog Card No. 98-71441
International Standard Book No.: 0-7641-0746-1

Printed in Hong Kong
9 8 7 6 5 4 3 2 1

Oscar
needs a
Friend

Oscar was a bear who couldn't keep still.
All day long he raced around the mountainside.

At bedtime he raced around Mom.

And when at last he snuggled down, Oscar
always said the same thing.
"I wish there were more bears on our side of
the mountain. And I wish there was another
bear who liked the same sort of games as I!"

Weeks passed and Oscar wondered if he would ever find a friend.

Then one day he bounded home, bursting
with excitement.

"Mom, Mom," cried Oscar. "Some new bears
have moved in . . . just up the track. And the
little one looks as if he needs a friend, too."

The new little bear was named Ollie. And
right after lunch Oscar set off to meet him.

"Let's play on my slide," said Oscar. And, without waiting for a reply, he pulled Ollie to the top of his favorite bank.

"Isn't this great!" cried Oscar, as the two bears tumbled down the bank together.

But Ollie wasn't so sure. And before long
he scurried back to his mom.

That evening at supper Oscar was sulky. But the next day he went to see Ollie again.

"Let's play on my bouncy branch," said Oscar. And, without waiting for a reply, he pushed Ollie up into his favorite tree.

"Isn't this great!" cried Oscar, as the
two bears tried to balance in the breeze.

But Ollie wasn't so sure. And before long he scurried back to his mom.

That night at story time Oscar stomped about.

But the next day he went to see Ollie again.
"Let's play hide-and-seek," said Oscar.

And, without waiting for a reply,
he ran off and left Ollie in the
dark and gloomy wood.

"Isn't this great!" hollered Oscar from
a distance. But Ollie was already wailing.
"I want to go home . . . *now*!"

That night at bedtime Oscar had a tantrum.

"Ollie says my slide's too steep, my branch
is too bouncy, and my wood's too scary,"
he yelled. "And he keeps running home to
his mom."

When at last she could make herself heard,
Oscar's mom made a suggestion.

Oscar pretended not to listen. But before
he went to sleep, he thought about what
Mom had said.

And the next morning he raced over to Ollie's home.

"What would *you* like to do today?" asked Oscar. Then he waited patiently for a reply.

At first there was a stunned silence. But next there was a *whoooosh!* And Ollie bounced out from behind his mom.

"Swimming!" he announced. And the two bears ran eagerly toward the water.
Oscar watched in amazement as Ollie scrambled up to the highest rock.
And leapt straight in.

"We had a huge lake at my old home,"
explained Ollie.

All morning the two bears splashed and
whooped in the water.

That afternoon Ollie asked if he could try
Oscar's slide again. And then his branch.
"It's easier than I thought," beamed Ollie.

"I do hope he'll want to play hide-and-seek soon," thought Oscar to himself. But he knew now that he must wait until Ollie was ready.

"And what do you think of your new friend today?" asked Mom, when it was time to take Ollie home.

"I think that Ollie is *brilliant*!" cried Oscar.
"And that I am the luckiest bear on the
mountain."